THE DISCOVERY

SCAN THE QR CODE ON THE BACK COVER
TO UNLOCK A SPECIAL MESSAGE FROM
ROBERT IRWIN

Other books in the
Robert Irwin, Dinosaur Hunter series:

THE DISCOVERY

WRITTEN BY JACK WELLS

RANDOM HOUSE AUSTRALIA

A Random House book
Published by Random House Australia Pty Ltd
Level 3, 100 Pacific Highway, North Sydney NSW 2060
www.randomhouse.com.au

First published by Random House Australia in 2013

The publisher would like to thank David Elliott from the Australian Age of
Dinosaurs.

Addresses for companies within the Random House Group can be found at
www.randomhouse.com.au/offices

National Library of Australia
Cataloguing-in-Publication Entry

Author: Irwin, Robert, 2003–
Title: The Discovery / Robert Irwin, Jack Wells.
ISBN: 978 1 86471 845 4 (pbk.)
Series: Robert Irwin dinosaur hunter; 1.
Target Audience: For primary school age children.
Subjects: Dinosaurs – Juvenile fiction.
Other Authors/Contributors: Kunz, Chris.
Dewey Number: A823.4

Cover and internal illustrations by Lachlan Creagh
Cover and internal design by Christabella Designs
Typeset by Midland Typesetters, Australia
Printed in Australia by Griffin Press, an accredited ISO AS/NZS 14001:2004
Environmental Management System printer

Random House Australia uses papers that are natural, renewable and recyclable
products and made from wood grown in sustainable forests. The logging
and manufacturing processes are expected to conform to the environmental
regulations of the country of origin.

CHAPTER ONE

The assassin focused in on his target. It was going to be easy. The target was concentrating so hard, there was no way he'd notice the stealthy footfalls of the assassin as he came at the target from behind. It was going to be the easiest job the assassin had had in ages. So easy,

in fact, he wondered if he should delay it until the target could at least put up a bit of a fight.

Nah, he'd destroy him now anyway.

Then he could go dirt bike riding.

The assassin crept closer and closer. The dinosaur mask he was wearing was getting hot, and the eyeholes kept moving. He could only hope the target was still in sight. He couldn't actually tell for sure. The target was using a handheld power tool, so there would be no way of hearing the assassin move with the stealth of a tiger and *the weightlessness of something really light – maybe a feather – yeah, a feather. The target would be mincemeat and not even know how he got minced, this assassin was that good.*

Two more footsteps and the target would be done, good and proper ...

Unexpectedly, the target turned around, brandishing what looked like a dentist's drill, and shouted 'Riiiiiiiillley!' really loud.

Riley the assassin jumped a mile into the air in fright.

His best friend Robert, aka the target,

howled with laughter. 'Awesome mask. Is it meant to be an *allosaurus*?'

Riley ripped off the mask. 'I don't know. I just picked it up at the museum shop. I thought I'd actually scare you this time.'

Robert smirked. 'Good luck with that, mate.'

'But I was sure I'd got you. You were so busy looking at that boring old rock.'

Robert was shocked. 'This is no boring old rock! This is the most exciting rock *ever*.'

Riley raised an eyebrow.

'C'mon, mate, you know what's inside this rock, don't you?'

'A whole lot of smaller rocks squashed together?' said Riley, playing dumb.

'Nup,' answered Robert. 'Inside this rock is a dinosaur fossil, which is what makes this rock so awesome. Didn't you listen when we went out with the palaeontologist this morning?'

'Kind of. Well, not really. Out the window I could see some excellent trails that would be good for dirt-biking.'

Robert was still holding the rock. He hadn't finished trying to convince

his friend of how amazing fossils were. 'Once upon a time, this fossil was a part of a real-life dinosaur that roamed prehistoric Australia. It might have been a huge carnivore the size of four elephants or a scrawny feathered herbivore the size of an oversized rooster. That's what I want to find out.'

Riley was still not convinced. 'Who cares? They lived ages ago.'

Robert grinned. 'Exactly. That's what makes it so exciting!'

'Speaking of exciting, wanna go

dirt bike riding?' asked his best friend, completely missing the point.

'Later. I just want to spend a bit more time with this guy,' said Robert, looking fondly at the rock in his hand. 'But if you find the best tracks, you can count on a race later on.'

Riley gave his mate a friendly whack on the back of the head with the dinosaur mask. 'You bet. And then you'll really be scared. Scared of my speed and skill!'

Robert smiled as Riley trudged out the door of the dinosaur fossil laboratory and into the glaring Queensland sunshine.

He turned to an impressive-looking figure in the corner of the lab – a large fossil of the leg of a titanosaur, which had been affectionately named Wade. The poor 'saur was currently missing a head, a tail and quite a few bits in-between, but the size of its leg made it clear that, once upon a time, this enormous dinosaur was probably the size of a small building!

'Wade, not everyone loves dinosaurs the way I do. I don't understand it, but I have to accept it. Now, if you're lucky, in this rock I might just uncover another piece of you. That'd be good, wouldn't it? I know you'd like to be more than just a large leg. Let's see if I can help you with that.'

Robert turned on the drill, which was actually called an air scribe, a specialised tool used to help remove rock from around fossils, and once again focused on his special task.

For Robert Irwin, life didn't get much better than this. Here he was in a dino laboratory in outback Australia, helping to uncover new fossils at the Australian Age of Dinosaurs – best birthday present ever!

CHAPTER TWO

A few weeks before Robert's ninth birthday, his mum had asked what he'd like most in the world. He didn't hesitate. He knew *exactly* what he wanted.

Robert lived with his mum and his sister, Bindi, at Australia Zoo, on Queensland's Sunshine Coast. It was a

fantastic place for a boy to grow up. He already knew he was one of the luckiest kids in the world, and although he really, really loved lots of living creatures, what Robert loved even more were creatures that had roamed the earth a long time ago: creatures with enormous tails and enormous teeth, creatures that ruled the world long before humans were around.

Dinosaurs.

Big ones, small ones, feathered ones, flying ones. It didn't matter. He loved them all.

After some serious organisation involving new tyres for the Land Cruiser, camping gear and a new bike rack for their dirt bikes, the Irwins, along with Robert's best friend, Riley, drove northwest for hours, away from the Queensland coast. Finally, they arrived at a small outback town called Winton, a place where some very exciting dinosaur discoveries had recently been made. It was also home to Australia's only museum dedicated to Australian dinosaurs.

Even after hours of driving, Robert was nowhere near running out of dinosaur facts. '... And in 1964 they discovered *Minmi paravertebra* (min-mee par-ah-ver-te-bra), an ankylosaur, a four-legged dinosaur with body armour. *Minmi* was the first ankylosaur found in the Southern Hemisphere.'

Riley looked over at his friend. 'How do you remember all this stuff?'

Robert shrugged. 'I just do. He was a cute little dino that lived in the early Cretaceous period, and was only about a metre tall.'

'So he wouldn't have eaten me?' asked Riley.

'No, I think he was a plant-eater. And judging by the fact that he was covered in armour, *minmi* looks like he was built to defend himself rather than attack others. Those armoured plates are called scutes, just like what crocs have.'

Robert knew a lot about crocodiles, because he was the son of the famous Crocodile Hunter, Steve Irwin, who had devoted his life to caring for animals, especially crocodiles, before his untimely death when Robert was still small. Apart from looking just like his dad, Robert also shared his adventurous spirit.

After their first night camping, Robert and Riley were up early the next morning to go out on a dig with a palaeontologist called Paul Battersby and a few other volunteers from the Queensland Museum. The dig site was about 40 kilometres outside Winton on a large sheep station. The area had already produced some important fossil finds and had been prepared, waiting for the small group to begin work. Robert was bursting with excitement!

They had brought a range of tools with them, from geo picks, rock hammers and

chisels, to a range of different brushes. This was hard, hot and exacting work, and you needed a lot of patience and concentration to work under these conditions. It was unusual for a 9-year-old to be allowed to dig in the first place, but Robert Irwin wasn't your normal 9-year-old. He had started writing letters to palaeontologists around the time other kids became interested in writing to Santa.

On the other hand, it didn't take Riley long to lose interest. He went off in search of termite mounds. 'Riley, mate, don't go

upsetting any more of the wildlife,' said Robert with a grin.

A day earlier, the two of them had found a meat ant nest near their camp site. Riley couldn't resist poking a stick into the nest, only to regret his decision seconds later as an army of ants ran up his stick and attacked. The angry red bites were still itching all up Riley's right arm.

'Yep, I know. Looking, not touching,' replied Riley with a serious nod. He wasn't going to inflict that kind of pain on himself again any time soon.

As the small group began to fossick around the area, they could feel the curious eyes of a few sheep in a nearby paddock. Humans did a whole lot of strange things, but the sheep could not make head nor woolly tail of what this group was up to!

For the first half hour, the group combed the area, occasionally stopping to dig if something caught their eye.

'I'm just going to check out this area over here,' Robert called out as he took a swig of water from his drink bottle. The sun was shining bright when his eye

caught sight of something. He wandered closer to an interesting clump of grass, and found an unusually shaped rock.

Could it be?

'Paul, come over here!' Robert tried to contain his excitement.

Paul was a veteran when it came to these digs. He'd been taking part in dinosaur discoveries for over 20 years, all over the world. With his sun-bleached blond hair and warm smile, he was a palaeontologist who never got tired of the excitement of a potential find. He strolled over and took a close look at the rock. 'I'm sorry, little guy,' he said, patting Robert on the back. 'Not this time.'

Robert grinned, undiscouraged. 'No worries.' And he immediately went back to scouring the ground once more.

Paul took off his hat and admired the boy's determination. 'You're a true-blue dinosaur hunter, you know that?'

Robert chuckled, not taking his eyes off the ground in front of him as he continued to scan the area. 'Yeah, just like my dad was the Crocodile Hunter, I'll be Robert Irwin the Dinosaur Hunter.'

'It definitely has a ring to it,' said Paul, with a chuckle.

Bailey, a volunteer, added, 'All you need to make it come true is to –'

'Hey, take a look at this!' With his geo pick, Robert dug carefully around what looked to be a partially buried boulder.

'– find a dinosaur,' Bailey finished with a grin.

Paul bent down to take a closer look at what Robert had unearthed. 'Ah, now *this* could be something special.'

Robert continued to carefully remove

the soil around the boulder. His geo pick tapped against something only a couple of centimetres away from a bigger boulder. Paul was smiling. 'Just dig really carefully around there ... Looks like it might be ...'

Robert changed from the pick to a largish brush, and carefully swept away the loose soil. 'A dinosaur claw?!'

Paul grinned. 'Yeah, I think you're right, Robert. Looks like it might be a claw. As well as some kind of much bigger fossil inside the boulder right next to it.'

Robert, wearing a grin the size of a crocodile's, stood up and raised both hands in the air like he'd just won an Olympic gold medal. 'I found a fossil. *Two* fossils. Doubly awesome!'

CHAPTER THREE

Robert's moment of triumph was interrupted by Riley limping back to the dig site, holding one of his feet and yelping in pain.

Robert rushed over to his friend in concern. 'What is it? A snake bite? Another meat ant attack?'

Riley shook his head. 'Nope.' He looked a little bashful. 'A bee sting.'

While one of the volunteers went off in search of the first aid kit, Robert sat with his friend at the edge of the dig site.

'We'll have to give you a new nickname, mate. Riley the Insect Aggravator,' suggested Robert with a straight face.

'I don't like that nickname.' Riley glared at his best friend before returning to watch his bee sting grow red and swell.

Robert thought it might be a good idea to change the subject. Perhaps now wasn't the time to pay out his friend, who was obviously in pain. 'Well, I've got a new nickname – it's Robert Irwin the Dinosaur Hunter. And I've just found dino fossils.'

Riley brightened at the news. 'That's awesome! What dinosaur do they belong to?'

Robert shrugged. 'I don't know yet. It actually takes months, sometimes even years, to work out which creature a fossil belongs to. It's like a massive jigsaw puzzle where you first have to work out which pieces belong to what puzzle.'

Riley yawned. He didn't have the

patience for jigsaw puzzles. 'Robert Irwin the Dinosaur Hunter's a beaut nickname.' He started feeling sorry for himself. 'I want a nickname like that.'

'How about Riley the Dirt Bike Champion?' suggested Robert, trying to make his friend feel better.

Riley smiled, warming to the idea immediately. 'Yeah, that'll do.'

Back at the lab, Robert was getting peckish. It was feeling like afternoon-snack time. He took out his digital voice

recorder and made a quick update.

'1600 hours on 10 March 2013. Lab work. After three hours using the air scribe, I've managed to uncover another five centimetres of fossil. I reckon I might be working on a femur, which is a thigh bone.' Robert turned to Wade in the corner. 'Sorry, Wade, I don't think you're going to get more body parts out of me today.'

Robert admitted to himself that it was frustrating it would take so long before the fossil he'd found this morning could be linked to an actual dinosaur. He couldn't stop thinking about the claw. Imagine if it was from his favourite dinosaur, *Australovenator wintonensis* (oss-tra-low-ven-ah-tor win-ton-en-sis)! But he wouldn't know for months, maybe even years.

He finished his update and slipped the recorder back into his jacket. For the past year, Robert had been recording all of his dinosaur adventures on his digital voice recorder, and was planning on putting together a journal of all his discoveries.

'Owww!' As he got up from his chair, Robert felt a sharp prod from the back

pocket of his shorts. He looked around. The lab was empty. Even before he could reach into his back pocket there was another sharp prod. 'Owww! What is *that*?' He reached into his shorts pocket and pulled out . . . a fossilised claw!

'Hang on, where did this come from?' He looked closely at the fossil. 'It could be the claw I found on the dig this morning. But how . . .?'

Once the claw had been carefully dug up, Robert had given the fossil to Paul, and it had been wrapped and loaded onto a truck with the other fossils found that day. Robert couldn't think of an explanation as to how it came to be in his back pocket.

He looked around at the deserted lab, and started to feel a bit dizzy. The walls of the laboratory looked like they were bending inwards, and the ground below him began to shimmer. He took hold of the fossil in both hands and, suddenly, the dizziness became a lot more intense, like he was getting dragged down a plughole really fast.

Robert managed to call out a weak 'Rillleeeeey . . .' before he blacked out.

CHAPTER FOUR

Robert rolled over and groaned. Since when was his bed this uncomfortable? It was definitely time for a new pillow. This one was hard and cold, and eeugh, was that moss tickling his nose? *Gross.* He slowly opened one eye, then the other, and surveyed his surroundings.

No, he wasn't in bed and this certainly wasn't his pillow. He got up from the mossy rock he'd been leaning on. It was deathly quiet. He was in a forested area – bushland somewhere – but he had no idea where.

Robert tried to remember how he'd got here. But nothing came to mind. How *had* he got here?

'Riley? Mum, are you here?' he called out groggily.

A slight wind whistled through the trees. Robert got the feeling there wasn't a single human being around for miles.

He shivered, wrapping his jacket around him for warmth.

Maybe he was dreaming. He vaguely remembered being in the fossil lab with Riley trying to sneak up on him. He wasn't even tired. Why would he have fallen asleep?

He looked around and found the fossilised claw lying next to the mossy rock. Without quite knowing why, he reached over gingerly and touched it with both hands. Nothing happened.

None of this made any sense at all.

All of a sudden the ground started to vibrate. Robert looked up in alarm. Where was he and what was happening? Was this an earthquake? Or an erupting volcano? He couldn't see a volcano from where he was but, right now, he wasn't about to rule anything out. It didn't feel like any dream he'd ever had before. This was far too real!

The trees and ferns around him were pulsing in time with the vibrations, and there was a sound, a sort of a dull thrum, which was building second by second.

Robert's intuition told him to get off the ground – and fast. He shoved the fossil back into his pocket to think about later, then raced to the nearest tree and started to climb.

Once he was a few metres above the ground, Robert stopped and settled himself onto a branch. The vibrations became more intense, and in the distance he could see a large dust cloud moving rapidly in his direction.

Robert had heard of the massive migrations that animals like wildebeest and antelope made every year in Africa, but he'd never seen one firsthand. Could he be in Africa?

His hands shook as got out his voice recorder. Whatever it was he was about to see, he wanted to make sure it was documented.

He checked his watch and saw the battery was dead. He must have bumped it when he blacked out. He pressed record on his digital voice recorder. 'Ummm, not sure how to start this entry. I'm somewhere, I don't know exactly where . . . I'm up a tree, watching a large dust cloud move closer and closer. The ground below me is shaking, and I have absolutely no idea what's coming my way.'

Robert held his breath. For now, there was nothing else to say.

CHAPTER FIVE

The sound of thunderous galloping was overwhelming. The dust was making it hard to see but it looked like a herd of . . .

Robert wiped the dust from his eyes and peered down into the cloud.

He almost fell out of the tree. *Dinosaurs?!*

He felt the fossil in his back pocket. 'I've travelled back in time?' This was impossible. Was someone going to come out from behind a tree and say 'Just kidding!'?

The herd was galloping past, along the dusty path below Robert's tree. They were fast, bird-like dinosaurs that ran on two legs. Real-life dinosaurs! Robert's brain churned through all the dinosaur info he had stored in his head. He thought they could be ornithopods. If he was right, they were herbivorous, which meant they were plant-eaters and posed no direct threat to him. Although, if he'd stayed on the ground, it wouldn't have been so comfortable getting stepped on by stampeding dinosaurs, even if they were small ones!

Once the dust cloud cleared, Robert coughed a little and took a few seconds to rub the dirt from his eyes, trying to remain quiet. He wasn't sure if the ornithopods were being chased or whether they were just travelling to a new location.

When the last one disappeared from sight, Robert waited until he was sure no predator was following the herd, then he climbed down from the tree and onto the dusty track.

Okay, so he had travelled back in time. This wasn't a dream or a practical joke. And it had to have something to do with the fossil he'd found. Even though he still felt dazed by the discovery, Robert realised that this was the chance of a lifetime. He wasn't going to waste time thinking about it. He had things to check out! Robert started jogging along

the path left by the ornithopod herd, excitement building in his chest.

As he ran, he recorded an update. 'Can you believe it? I reckon that somehow I've ended up in prehistoric Australia, possibly some time in the Cretaceous period. It's incredible. I've just seen my first herd of dinosaurs. I think the group were ornithopods, which are about the size of emus. They're herbivores, they walk on two legs and travel in packs.'

Robert looked around as the landscape began to change. He was

leaving the forest behind and could see that a clearing lay ahead. Travelling a few steps further, he paused when he found the pack had stopped to drink from a muddy riverbank. He crouched down, lowering his voice to a whisper.

'Within the group, it looks like there are both adults and juveniles. The river they're drinking from is probably familiar to them, as they seemed to know the direction they were heading in. And they're not the only species using the river as a watering hole. I'm going to take a closer look.'

Robert snuck as close as he thought was safe, his shoes sinking slightly into the muddy soil. 'Crikey, I think the other dinosaurs may be coelurosaurs. Amazing creatures! They're brown and leathery with long necks and small beady eyes. They're known to be carnivorous, which means they're meat-eaters, but they don't seem interested in taking a bite out of the ornithopods. They're a smaller species. In fact – take a look at that – I can see a few of the coelurosaurs snapping at insects near the water's edge. Smaller food items, like frogs or small reptiles, are probably more within their reach.'

Robert stopped recording and took a deep breath. What had started off as a really good birthday present – a dinosaur dig and fossil preparation – had just become a million times better! This present had become totally out of this world! If only Riley could see it as well – then he'd understand how awesome dinosaurs really were!

When Robert could bear to tear his eyes away from the dinosaurs, he took a closer look at the surrounding environment. It was a much cooler climate here than it had been in the hot sun of present-day Winton. He was lucky he'd kept his jacket on while he'd been in the lab. And there were no gum trees or grass here now. He knew that cycads, gingko trees and various different types of fern were a part of Australia in the Cretaceous period, but to see them with his own eyes was just incredible!

All of a sudden, an enormous roar ripped through the air. Robert stifled a yelp and sprinted as fast as he could into the relative safety of the bushland. He hid, shaking, behind a small tree fern at the edge of the clearing.

His heart was pounding.

Of course, it was fine to get excited about living in the time of dinosaurs, but the tricky thing was working out how to stay alive when there were so many enormous, meat-eating giants roaming the place!

CHAPTER SIX

Robert wasn't the only one alarmed by the terrifying sound. The herd of dinosaurs drinking by the stream panicked. They stampeded in all directions, causing mayhem, squealing and braying as they tried to gallop out of harm's way.

Despite his fear, Robert knew he had to get a look at the creature that could produce a roar like that. He inched his way to a position, still half-hidden by fern fronds, where he could watch the drama unfold.

And then the beast appeared. On two legs, scaly and terrifying, the creature let out another bellow. His gleaming rows of razor-like teeth were making it clear to the smaller dinosaurs that they were most definitely on the menu! Robert couldn't believe his luck. He had to remind himself to breathe. 'I think this

guy ... this guy is an *australovenator*. It's incredible to see him in the flesh. He's called the Southern Hunter and he's absolutely fearsome. He's a carnivore. And I reckon it's just about lunchtime. There's no doubt about it. The smaller dinos know this and are running for their lives.'

The *australovenator* ran towards the group of smaller dinosaurs, causing them to scramble, some sprinting away from the creature and, strangely, some running straight towards it. It was like watching an unusual prehistoric game of chicken. The small 'saurs were much quicker than the hungry theropod, but the size of his claws made Robert believe the *australovenator* would not leave the river's edge with an empty stomach!

CHAPTER SEVEN

The stampede was over in moments. The *australovenator* was able to grab hold of a coelurosaur that had become trapped on the mudflats and, with a swipe of his claws, the smaller dinosaur was dead. And seconds after that, it had been eaten. This carnivore wasted

no time on good table manners.

Robert pressed record and whispered, 'This is just the first course for a dinosaur of this size. I'd better make sure I don't move a muscle until he's well on his way to finding his next course! Hopefully his dessert is waiting for him a couple of kilometres away.'

None of the coelurosaurs or ornithopods had hung around to watch the quick feast. The dinosaur shook his head and bellowed. 'Did I just hear a dinosaur burp?' wondered Robert, and watched as the beast slowly loped down

to the edge of the riverbank and back the way he had come.

Robert realised his heart was still thumping in his chest. The creature was terrifying ... and incredible! He waited until his heartbeat had returned to normal and his hands had stopped shaking, then he waited a few more minutes to make sure the theropod was long gone before deciding to emerge from his hiding place.

Taking a deep breath, Robert looked around. His legs were still a bit shaky. It was now eerily quiet. All that remained were hundreds of dinosaur tracks in the mud. Robert walked down to the water's edge and pressed record once more on his voice recorder.

'Although it's incredible to be here, I'm starting to wonder just how or if I can get back to my life in 2013.' He felt scared and alone. Surviving in this harsh environment would be really hard, maybe even impossible. Where could he find a place to stay safe and uneaten? What would he eat? He imagined grabbing hold of vines and swinging through the forest like Tarzan, trying to escape the

claws of countless terrifying creatures. If he could find a *minmi*, he could maybe make friends with it. They could set up camp together. And chances are it wouldn't be as accident prone as Riley. But it probably wouldn't crack jokes either. Robert grimaced. If he was stuck here, it would be hard . . . and lonely. He swallowed the lump that had formed in his throat.

'You'll be all right, mate,' he said to himself, trying to cheer himself up. 'Who knows what might happen to Riley if I'm not there to save him from his next insect attack?' Pulling the fossilised claw from his back pocket, Robert stared at it for a moment. 'How do I get back home?' he asked in a quiet voice. He waited a few moments but the fossil didn't answer. He sighed.

And behind him, he heard another sigh, which was more like a snort. Turning around slowly, Robert found himself staring into the face of another *australovenator*, a smaller version of the earlier scary one. Although, admittedly, this one was still pretty scary!

It had leant down to give Robert a

sniff. This was the first time it had come across a creature like this!

For a dinosaur that might have weighed around 350 kilograms, he was surprisingly light on his feet. Robert hadn't heard a thing.

His heart thumped hard against his rib cage. He was too scared to breathe. On the one hand, Robert was thrilled – his favourite dinosaur was so close he could touch him.

Robert's scientific brain, even under this much stress, couldn't help cataloguing the amazing specimen in front of him:

the long claws and its razor-sharp teeth. It was a mottled colour. Brown and a little reddish. The claws looked strikingly similar to the fossilised one Robert held in his hand. He was pretty sure he no longer needed to wait for confirmation that he'd discovered an *australovenator* claw back in modern-day Australia – the proof was right here in front of him. The 'proof' also had really bad breath. Now *that* was something that was never mentioned in dinosaur museums!

On the other hand, the *australove-nator* was called the Southern Hunter for a good reason. This was a bloodthirsty carnivorous dinosaur, and even though this one was young, Robert couldn't help thinking that he just might get to feel the strength of the dino's jaws firsthand . . . any second now.

Luckily, it seemed that Robert was not a food source the young theropod was familiar with, and the dinosaur was still hesitating.

Robert didn't know what to do. Instinct told him he shouldn't run. Instead, he raised the fossilised claw. 'Look, mate,' he spoke in a husky voice.

'Do you reckon this claw could've belonged to you or one of your family?'

The *australovenator* leant even closer to Robert's face. Robert tried not to offend the dinosaur by screwing up his nose but he couldn't help thinking, 'Man, if I had a mint, I'd offer it. This guy has seriously not brushed his teeth for a century!' Luckily, the dino couldn't mind-read.

The *australovenator* glared at Robert for a second longer, took a sniff of the fossil, stood up to his full towering height and let out an almighty roar.

CHAPTER EIGHT

The force of the noise hurled Robert, who was still clutching the fossilised claw, into the lapping water of the river's edge. It was cold! He struggled to find his footing on the muddy bank but was then overwhelmed by a wave of dizziness. What was happening now? Taking a

deep breath, Robert blinked his eyes in an attempt to focus them. The dizziness increased. The *australovenator* turned to take one last look at Robert before roaring once more and bounding off in the same direction the larger dinosaur had gone.

After what felt like seconds later but was in actual fact millennia later, Robert opened his eyes and found himself back in the laboratory. He was soaking wet, and holding on tightly to

the fossil. The lab was empty, although he could hear Riley calling him from outside.

'Robert, I've eaten six scones already and I'll take the last three if you don't come and get 'em in the next 10 seconds. 10 . . . 9 . . . 8 . . . 7 . . . 6 . . .'

It was so good to hear his friend's voice. Robert blinked and checked he had two arms, two legs and his head was still on top of his neck.

His stomach rumbled. A scone or three sounded good. Dinosaur hunting built up an appetite, that was for sure!

Robert stood up, feeling dazed but exhilarated. He had no explanation of how it had happened, or why it had happened, but he knew it really *had* happened.

This was no strange dream or hallucination. The fossil he was holding was special, and it had chosen him. And it had helped answer Robert's question about who the dinosaur claw had belonged to. This was a magic fossil and he knew he'd have to keep it safe.

'You'd better leave me some scones,

Riley, or there'll be trouble,' Robert shouted, wondering how he was going to explain how he'd come to be so wet. 'I'm starving!'

CHAPTER NINE

The next day the Irwin family and Riley travelled south of Winton to a place called Lark Quarry Conservation Park.

Today they were taking a tour around the largest recorded dinosaur stampede in the world. This was the last day of the Robert Irwin Birthday Spectacular, and

Robert was still buzzing from yesterday's birthday surprise! He still wasn't quite sure what this now meant for him. Would it happen again? Did he have any control over where or when he would travel back in time? It was thrilling but also pretty scary at the same time.

To explain away his wet clothing, Robert had made a lame joke about dodgy bathroom plumbing when he met up with Riley and his family outside the laboratory and, bizarrely, they had believed him.

The tour group moved on to another

part of the exhibit as the guide explained that palaeontologists had worked out that a large theropod had appeared by the river's edge, frightening a group of ornithopods and coelurosaurs, causing the stampede to occur.

And because it had rained a few days after the event, the water from the river had risen and covered the dino tracks with a sandy sediment, preserving the dramatic event of millions of years ago.

It all sounded very, very familiar to Robert.

Riley was impressed. 'I think I'm starting to see why you like dinosaurs so much, Robert. It's pretty sweet that these guys can tell what happened just by looking at some old tracks. And from such a long time ago. Imagine what it would've been like back then!'

Robert turned to his friend. 'Those guys were really scared, you know. The *australovenator* was terrifying.'

Riley gave him a quizzical look. 'Hang on, the guide didn't say anything about it being an austrowhatsisname. I think he just called it a theropod.'

'Oh, right. Well, I reckon it *could've* been an *australovenator*.'

Riley nodded. 'Knowing you and the stuff you read about dinosaurs all the time instead of dirt-biking with me, you're probably right.'

'Yeah, maybe.' Robert looked back at the hundreds of track marks in the display.

The reassuring prod that came from his back pocket made it clear that keeping his new discovery a secret was the right thing to do.

For now.

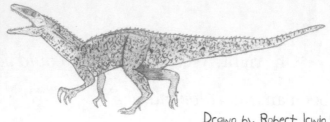

Drawn by Robert Irwin

AUSTRALOVENATOR

SCIENTIFIC NAME: Australovenator wintonensis

DISCOVERED: June 2006 in the Winton
Formation, central western
Queensland

ETYMOLOGY: Winton's Southern Hunter

PERIOD: Mid-Cretaceous, 100-98 million
years ago

LENGTH: Approximately 5 metres long

HEIGHT: Approximately 1.5 metres
tall at the hip

WEIGHT: Approximately 500 kilograms

Nicknamed 'Banjo' after the Australian poet Banjo Paterson, *Australovenator* is Australia's most complete skeleton of a carnivorous (meat-eating) dinosaur. Among the fossils discovered are nine teeth, both lower jaws, some ribs and bones belonging to the dinosaur's forearms, thigh, shins and feet.

Judging from its dimensions, *australovenator* was built for speed. Palaeontologists also found finger and wrist bones along with a middle claw that revealed hands close to 50 centimetres long that could spread to a whopping 30 centimetres wide at the tip of its claws! This means that Banjo would have had a massive grasping capability.

By scanning the fossils and then creating a mirror image of them through the use of 3D-imaging technology, experts were able to create an image of two complete forearms, which can be used to work out exactly how australovenator attacked its prey. It is believed that australovenator would have dug its mighty claws into its prey, holding it in an iron grip, before going in for the kill.

PREHISTORIC AUSTRALIA

When dinosaurs roamed the earth, Australia was part of the supercontinent, Gondwana. It was made up of most of the landmasses in today's Southern

Hemisphere, including Australia, Antarctica, Africa, South America and India.

Most of the dinosaur fossils found in Australia belong to the Cretaceous period (146–65 million years ago). During this time the Australian part of Gondwana was close to the South Pole. Australia had a temperate and humid climate, and for several weeks of each year, southern parts of Australia, such as Victoria, may have had an icy polar winter that included semi-darkness.

Towering conifer forests covered much of Australia during the Cretaceous period, and there were also smaller plants such as ferns, gingkoes, cycads, clubmosses and horsetails. This period of Australia's history also saw the appearance of the first flowering plants.

Most Australian dinosaurs have been found in the eastern half of Australia (Queensland, New South Wales and Victoria), though isolated dinosaur bones have also been unearthed in Western Australia and South Australia. Queensland, in particular, is a dinosaur hotspot, with two-thirds of the state being covered by Cretaceous rock.

THE AUSTRALIAN AGE OF DINOSAURS MUSEUM OF NATURAL HISTORY

Australian Age of Dinosaurs Inc. was formed in Winton, Queensland in August 2002.

Since then they have organised annual dinosaur digs in western Queensland, primarily in collaboration with the Queensland Museum. This has led to the discovery and recovery of what is now the world's largest collection of Australian dinosaur fossils.

In July 2006, they opened a fossil preparation facility, and in 2009 they announced to the world the discovery of three new species of Australian dinosaurs.

Banjo (carnivorous theropod) and Matilda and Clancy (giant plant-eating sauropods) were found in a vast geological deposit near Winton that dates from 98–95 million years ago.

The meat-eating *Australovenator wintonensis* (Banjo) has been coined Australia's answer to *Velociraptor*.

Palaeontologists say that *Diamantinasaurus matildae* (Matilda) was a solid and robust animal, filling a niche similar to the hippopotamus today.

The second new species, *Wintonotitan wattsi* (Clancy) represented a tall animal that may have been Australia's prehistoric answer to the giraffe.

New fossil beds are discovered each year in the Winton Formation, proving that there has never been a more exciting time for Australian palaeontology.

Interested in finding out what Robert does when he's not hunting for dinosaurs?
Check out www.australiazoo.com.au

COLLECT THE SERIES

THE DISCOVERY

AMBUSH AT CISCO SWAMP

ARMOURED DEFENCE

THE DINOSAUR FEATHER

AND LOOK OUT FOR BOOKS 5–8
COMING SOON!